look
once

look
twice

by janet marshall

Houghton Mifflin Company
Boston

To Linda and Derek

Copyright © 1995 by Janet Marshall

All rights reserved.
For information about permission
to reproduce selections from this book,
write to Permissions, Houghton Mifflin Company,
215 Park Avenue South, New York, New York 10003.

Manufactured in Singapore
Book design by David Saylor
The text of this book is set in 36 point Helvetica Black
The illustrations are cut paper, reproduced in full color.

TWP 10 9 8 7 6 5 4 3

Library of Congress Cataloging-in-Publication Data
Marshall, Janet.
Look once, look twice / by Janet Marshall.
p. cm.   ISBN 0-395-71644-6
1. English language—Alphabet—Juvenile literature.
[1. Alphabet.] I. Title.
PE1155.M367 1995   [E]—dc20
[421'.1]   94-27259   CIP   AC

Patterns are everywhere in the natural world: on fish and flowers, fruits and vegetables, animals and insects, in the sky and in the water. Look carefully at the patterns on the letters in this book. Each is a close-up view of something from nature. The letter is the clue. Look once, look twice—and guess what the pattern comes from.

asparagus

butterfly

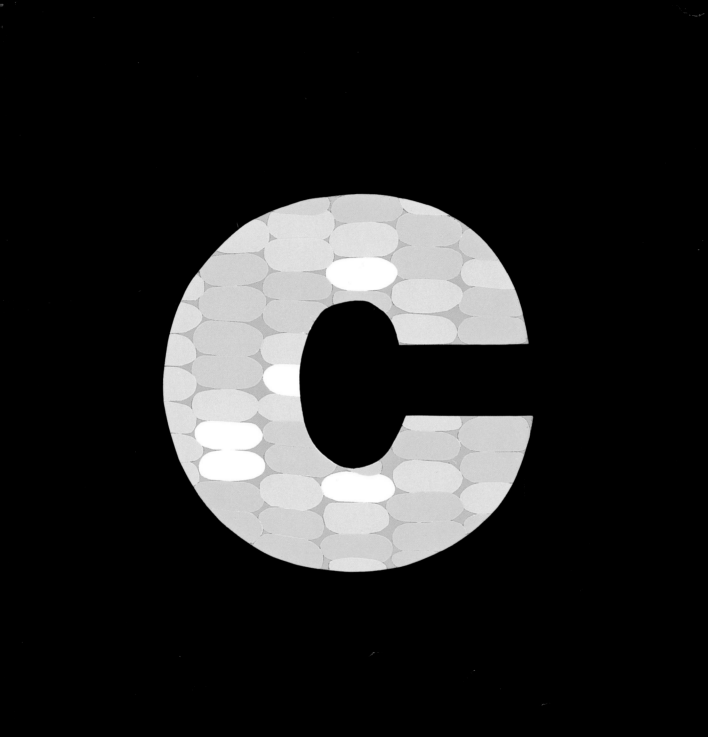

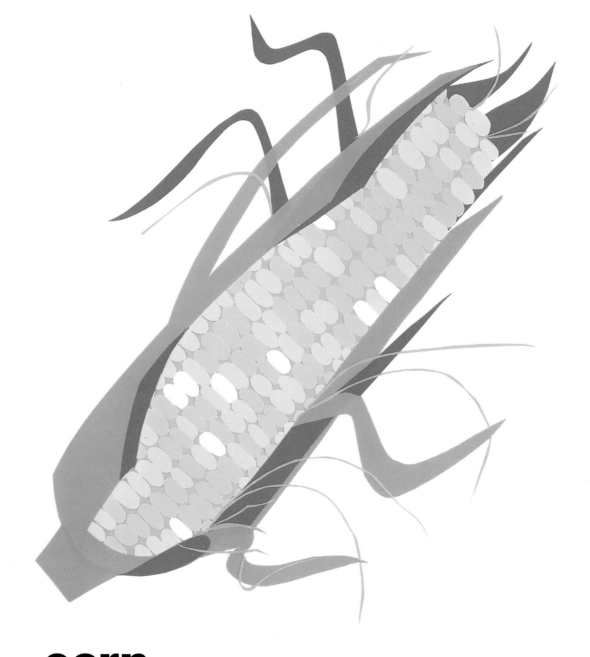

corn

dalmatian

eagle

fern

giraffe

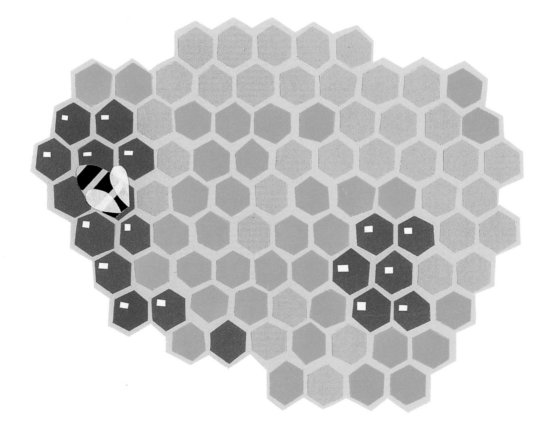

honeycomb

iris

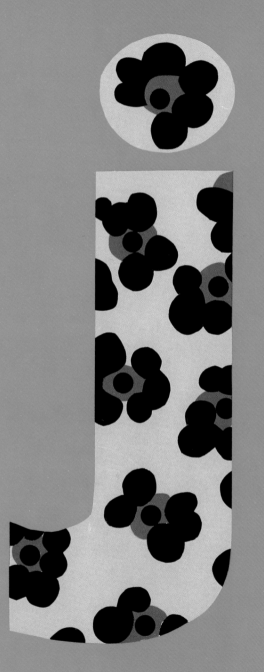

jaguar

kingfisher

ladybug

macaw

narcissus

ocean

pineapple

quail

rainbow

strawberry

tiger

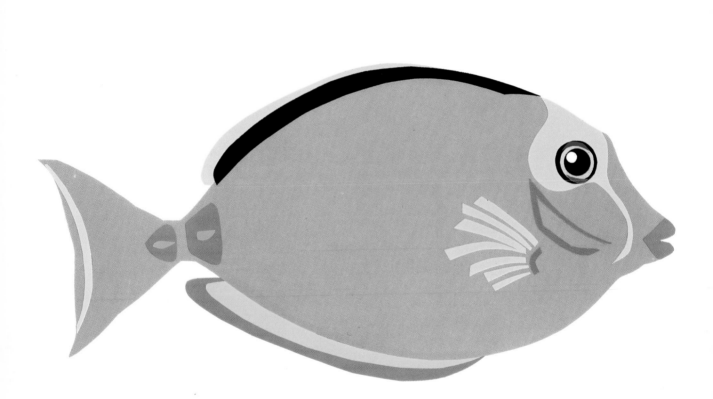

unicornfish

viper

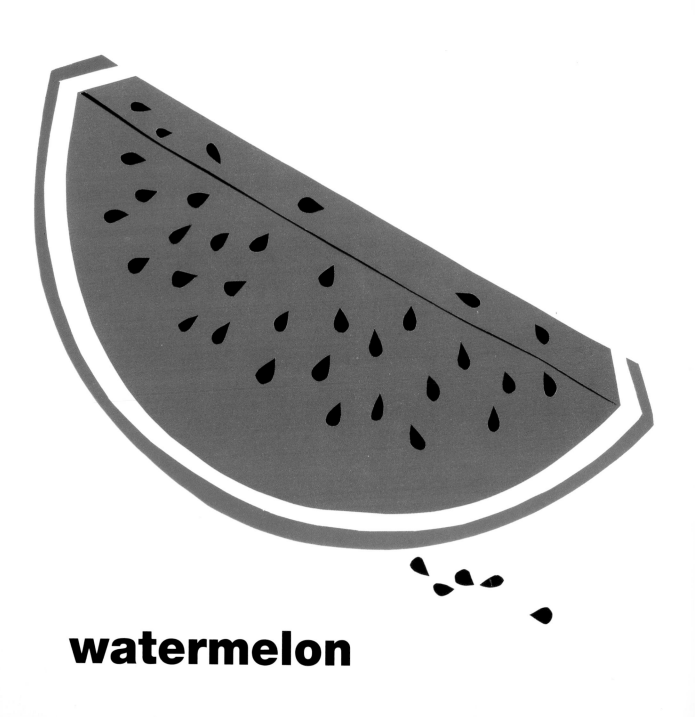

watermelon

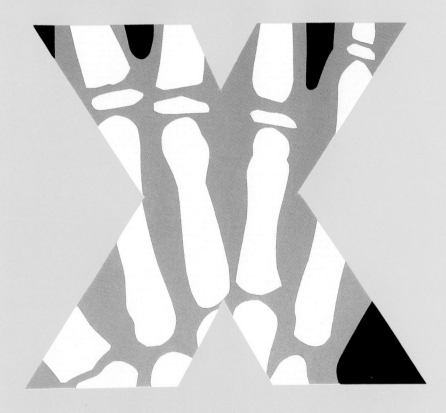

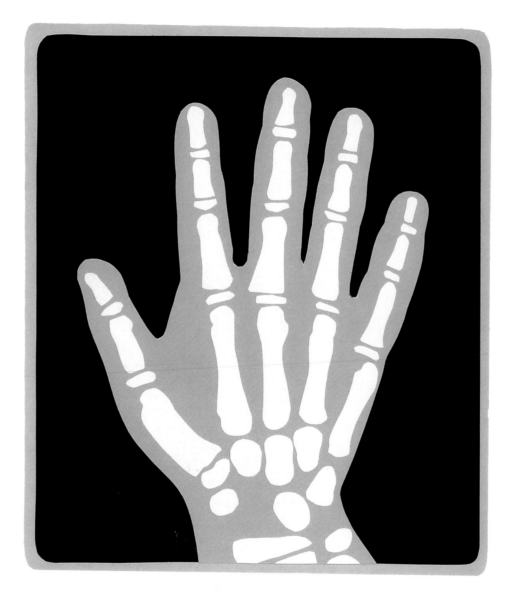

x-ray

yellow jacket

zebra